This book
belongs to

To Harry and Jenna, with love

FREDERICK WARNE

Published by the Penguin Group
Penguin Books Ltd, 80 Strand, London WC2R oRL, England
Penguin Young Readers Group, 345 Hudson Street,
New York, New York 10014, U.S.A.
Penguin Books Australia Ltd, 250 Camberwell Road, Camberwell,
Victoria 3124, Australia
Canada, India, New Zealand, South Africa

1

ISBN-13: 978 0 72325 840 7

Printed in Great Britain

Buttercup and the Fairy Gold

by Pippa le Quesne

Welcome to the Flower Fairy Garden!

Where are the fairies?
Where can we find them?
We've seen the fairy-rings
They leave behind them!

Is it a secret
No one is telling?
Why, in your garden
Surely they're dwelling!

No need for journeying,
Seeking afar:
Where there are flowers,
There fairies are!

Contents

Chapter One
A Surprise Shower

"This way! Quick!"

Buttercup gasped as a huge drop of rain hit her squarely on the head and then trickled down either side of her face.

She turned and set off for the top end of the meadow, where she knew there was an enormous dock plant growing. It was hard going, running uphill with the rain in her eyes, and Cowslip, who had longer legs, soon caught up. The two Flower Fairies took the last few strides side by side, mindful of the water trickling off the tips of the dock leaves and collecting

1

in murky pools on the ground.

"We're drenched!" exclaimed Cowslip as she lifted a strap over her head and carefully lowered two acorn-shell pots to the ground. Then she burst out laughing as she glanced at her friend.

Buttercup's flaxen hair was plastered to her head, her green stockings and shoes were speckled with mud, and her wings hung limply behind her. She grinned back at Cowslip but was preoccupied with examining the horse-chestnut shell that she had been carrying. When the first drop of rain had plopped on to her nose, Buttercup had plucked some petals and hastily covered her basket. Now she cautiously peeled one back and let out a sigh of relief as she caught sight of the gleaming pile of soft pollen.

Phew! It was safe—and the morning's work hadn't been wasted.

"It's only a shower, and once the sun's out, we'll soon dry off," she said cheerfully, leaning back against the sturdy stalk of the dock.

The huge plant towered way above them, and the two friends were silent for a few minutes, catching their breath and listening to the rain drumming

on the broad leaves overhead. Even though it was early summer, it had been hot for the past month or so, and the Flower Fairies knew that *everyone* would be glad of this shower.

"Lucky that we'd nearly finished," remarked Cowslip. She jumped to her feet and then, opening her tawny wings, began to beat them rapidly to get rid of any remaining water. Next she combed through her dark wavy hair with her fingers and shook out her layered yellow skirt.

"You're right," Buttercup agreed, absentmindedly spreading her own wings to let them drip dry. "Harvesting wet pollen is a nightmare. It's impossible to

stop it from sticking together in clumps."
She hugged her knees happily.

They'd been up since dawn, and she'd
already managed to visit nearly every one
of the buttercups in the meadow where
they lived. And that meant she must have
collected enough of her flowers' pollen to
keep her stocked up for practically the whole
year! All that was left to do was grind it up
to make her own special fairy dust and find
somewhere secret to store it.

"Wow, I'm
starving
after all that
work," said
Cowslip,
who had
just finished
wiping off
her bare legs

and feet with a scrap of the spongy moss that she'd used to seal her acorn pots. She reached into her skirt pocket and produced a piece of pale yellow honeycomb. "Here—let's share this. It's from Honeysuckle. The bees always

give him some in exchange for his flower nectar."

They'd been so absorbed in their harvesting that Buttercup hadn't noticed how hungry she was. Her tummy suddenly rumbled and reminded her that breakfast had, in fact, been hours ago. "Ooh, thanks. I've never tried it before," she said, gratefully taking the chunk of honeycomb that Cowslip held out to her. As soon as she bit into it, the sugary crystals melted on her tongue and filled her mouth with a sweetness more wonderful than anything she could remember tasting. Buttercup was so lost in the sensation that at first she didn't notice that the sound of pouring rain had been replaced by a soft tinkling that was gradually getting louder.

"Come and listen!" called Cowslip, who, with her acorn pots slung over her shoulder, had ventured out from their dock-leaf shelter.

From the top of the sloping meadow you could see the patchwork of farmers' fields that bordered the nearby woodland and the long, straight lane that cut across them.

Buttercup shielded her eyes from the already bright sunshine and peered in the direction that Cowslip was pointing. She couldn't see anything apart from a few birds fluttering in and out of the hedgerows, but coming from the lane was the distinct sound of fairy bells ringing. It was a familiar and welcome sound to them both as it heralded the arrival of one of their dearest friends. She always carried a long, slender stem that held snowy white flowers that nodded and tinkled as she walked.

"Lily-of-the-Valley!" Buttercup shouted happily. "Let's go and surprise her." And without waiting for a response, she bounded down the hill.

Chapter Two
Lost!

"It's *got* to be here somewhere!"

Buttercup had been around the dock plant in both directions and foraged through a tangle of nearby bindweed even though she knew she hadn't been anywhere near it. Now she was poking around in a murky puddle with a twig.

"Oh goodness, oh goodness—what if I've lost all that pollen?" she muttered to herself as she searched.

It wasn't just the heat of the sun that was making Buttercup feel uncomfortably hot. Nor was it the fact that when Lily had headed off home and Cowslip had gone for a nap, she'd remembered her horse-chestnut basket and run all the way back to the dock plant. No, it was because losing her morning's work meant that she wouldn't be able to make any more fairy dust. And, worse than that, the pollen falling into the wrong hands could have disastrous consequences!

It was hopeless, though, tiring herself out by running around in circles looking for it when, in her heart of hearts, the Flower Fairy knew that it was gone. She remembered putting down the basket and checking the pollen just before Cowslip had given her the honeycomb, then they had heard Lily's bells and, as soon as she had recognized them, Buttercup had run off down the meadow without a backward glance. Yup, she had definitely left it behind, and it looked certain that someone had come across it and taken it away.

But who? And where were they now? And how on earth would she begin to find them without any fairy dust? Fairy dust enabled each of the Flower Fairies to work a little magic—not conjure huge spells, but it was a helping hand in times of need. Yet not only had Buttercup completely run out, but now she was faced with the prospect of none at all until a new crop of flowers blossomed in the meadow.

Her heart started to beat very fast, and the young Flower Fairy felt quite overwhelmed by this thought.

"If only Cowslip were here—she'd make me feel better," Buttercup said out loud, thinking about her practical friend. Cowslip was very down-to-earth and always knew what to do. "I could go and find her ... but there's no time to lose," she went on. "No, I must try and work out exactly what she would do and sort this out by myself."

Buttercup walked to the brow of the hill and took a couple of deep breaths. She needed to focus her thoughts. She needed a plan. She gazed out across the fields and down at the lane below, and then, suddenly, an idea came to her.

"Jack! Jack! Are you there?"

Buttercup had come to the shady part of the lane where the tall jack-by-the-hedge plants, with their large green leaves and small white flowers, bordered the hedgerow. The Flower Fairy that tended them was never easy to find since his white shirt and breeches, green jerkin, and pearly wings camouflaged him well. It was this very fact that had given Buttercup the idea to come and seek him out. As the slender fairy was so hard to spot, passersby rarely knew of his presence, and so he picked up a lot of information as he went about his daily business.

Maybe he'd gone to visit the Flower Fairies Garden at the end of the lane. She'd keep looking for a few more minutes, then perhaps that was where she should go, too, and ask for the other fairies' help. But that would mean admitting just how careless she'd been with something so precious. Buttercup gulped.

At that moment, a flash of auburn caught her eye. *Jack?* And then, sure enough, out of the hedgerow popped just the face she was looking for, with its characteristic playful grin and red hair.

"Oh, I'm so pleased to see you, Jack," she gushed. "Um, I've misplaced something, and I wondered if you could help? It's my horse-chestnut basket. You wouldn't happen to have noticed anyone passing by this way and carrying one, would you? Oh—and how are you?" Buttercup blushed, suddenly realizing how rude she was, babbling away without even stopping to see how Jack was.

"I'm fine, thanks. Although, actually"—Jack stepped out of the hedge and leaned in close—"between you and me, something rather worrying happened not ten minutes ago."

Buttercup's stomach lurched.

"Go on," she said, trying not to let her voice tremble.

"Well, as long as you keep it to yourself ... Oh, and I'm waiting for a dragonfly to take me to the marshes, so as soon as one turns up I'll have to be off—"

"I absolutely promise." Buttercup beamed her most reassuring smile.

Jack nodded and hopped up on to his plant, where he patted the leaf next to him. "Best stay out of sight," he said. Then, after waiting for Buttercup to join him, he went on.

"What it is, you see—a couple of elves came by about a quarter of an hour ago. They were in an absolute frenzy of excitement and were talking loudly about some 'fairy gold' that they'd found. Now as you and

I well know, there's no such thing as fairy gold—that's just a human fable. But they were ever so pleased with their find and were deciding what to do with it. They seemed pretty sure that they could use it to 'buy' themselves some fairy secrets. That's when I really pricked up my ears. Then one of them said that he'd heard there was a Flower Fairy fair tonight, it being a full moon and all. He suggested that they disguise themselves as a couple of us, go along to the fair, and see how they could get the 'gold' to work in their favor. He felt sure they'd find out all sorts and maybe even leave with some special fairy magic.

"Now, I have no idea

what exactly it is that they found—because I stayed well out of sight—and it may well be totally harmless, but I reckon it's better to be safe than sorry. That's why I'm off to warn Kingcup and Queen of the Meadow that Flower Fairyland may be in real peril. If that dragonfly doesn't turn up in a minute then I'll just have to set off for the marshes on foot."

At that moment, Buttercup, who was deep in thought and had listened to every word with absolute horror, snapped herself out of her trance.

"No . . . no, Jack, it's fine." She spoke slowly so as not to convey the panic that was rising up inside her. "I know what they were talking about, and it really is no problem. It's all a silly misunderstanding and nothing to worry anyone else about. You know what the elves are like—they probably *knew* that

you were listening and
were trying to trick you."

She took a deep breath. "So I'll catch up
with them—and if I'm wrong I'll be certain
to get some help. And"—she paused, making
her mind up on the spot—"I'm going to the
fair tonight, anyway, so I can make doubly
sure that they don't get up to any mischief.
Okay?"

Then, without really giving Jack a
moment to reply, she jumped down from
her perch. He looked pretty perplexed by
her forceful speech, but Buttercup decided
that acting confidently might do the trick to
convince him. So, after waving good-bye,
she began to stride off purposefully down
the lane. And, when she dared to look back,
she saw that although Jack was shaking his
head in confusion, he was sending away the
dragonfly that had just turned up.

Chapter Three
Fairy Gold

As Buttercup fluttered away, she tried to make sense of the tangle of thoughts in her head. Her heart had skipped a beat when Jack-by-the-Hedge uttered the words "fairy gold." You see, although pretty much everyone in Flower Fairyland would tell you that there was no such thing, she knew differently.

Every summer when Buttercup's flowers blossomed, she would painstakingly polish the bright yellow petals

until the whole meadow shone with a carpet of dazzling gold. Then, obeying the most important Flower Fairy rule and keeping herself hidden, she would wait for her special visitors—humans.

Buttercup's wings ached, and the glowworm lantern that she'd hooked over her arm felt very heavy. Added to that, it was tiring concentrating on where she was going and trying to work on a plan at the same time. Oh, how she wished she was whiling away an afternoon watching the children playing.

Not far to the woodland now, she told herself, checking her progress. *You can do it!*

On more than one occasion she'd seen a child pick one of her bowl-shaped flowers and hold it up under another's chin. Apparently, if the gold reflected on their skin it meant that they liked butter. This always made Buttercup giggle, since she didn't even know what butter was!

"Gold knots, meadow cup, cuckoo flower . . . Gold knots, meadow cup, cuckoo flower," she recited, finding that it helped her focus her mind as she flew.

These were the different names that humans called her flowers. But mostly, because they longed to meet the magical creatures that lived among them, they made up stories about the fairies, and their favorite name for buttercups was 'fairy gold'.

At that moment, Buttercup touched down on the ground and, just as she did, a thought popped into her head. "If I know those crafty elves, they've been spying," she said out loud. "And I bet when they came across my basket of pollen, they thought they'd hit the jackpot."

She was standing on the edge of the woodland now, looking around for the clump of red-and-white toadstools that marked the path she needed to take.

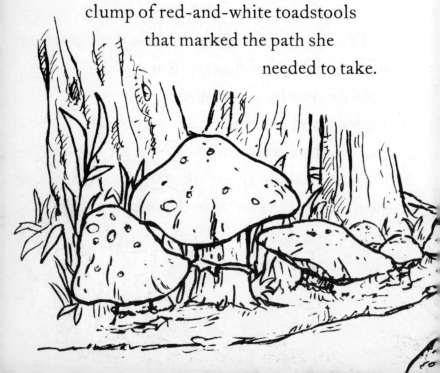

The thought of the elves having in their possession something so dear to her was just too awful.

"But then," she said, as it slowly dawned on her, "they don't know that it makes fairy dust, and that's more precious than anything they could possibly imagine!"

This was a closely guarded secret that only the Flower Fairies knew, and one that the elves were yet to discover. All of a sudden, she felt much better, and having located the spotted toadstools, Buttercup set off through the trees.

The monthly fair took place in a secret glade, and although she'd never been before, she knew how to find it. It was said to be a wonderful occasion, similar to the daily market where the Flower Fairies traded and sold their wares, but special because it took place after dark and only on the night of the full moon. Also, there was lively music and dancing to look forward to. But best of all, both Kingcup and Queen of the Meadow were rumored to always make an appearance.

Lily-of-the-Valley had recently gone along for the first time, and she'd come back bubbling over with enthusiasm. She'd promised Buttercup that as soon as she was old enough to stay up all night, the two of them would go together *every* month. Now Buttercup was not only going to the fair but she was finding her way there all by herself! As the little Flower Fairy jogged along the path, she couldn't help but feel a tingle of excitement.

Buttercup shivered and pulled the oak-leaf wrap more tightly about her. *There's nothing to*

be scared of, she
told herself.

The rain
shower had
given way
to another
scorching
day, but once
the sun sunk
below the horizon, it had turned into a cool,
cloudless evening. She'd put on the cloak
to hide her striking butterfly wings and
distinctive gold dress from the sharp-eyed
elves, and now she was glad of the extra
layer.

Buttercup stood at the mouth of the
tunnel that ran through the center of a
thicket and indicated the final leg of her
journey. Her lantern only produced a
very soft light, and as she peered into the

passageway, all she could see was inky blackness.

"On the other side of this is the fair, where there'll be lots of friendly faces." Buttercup took a deep breath. "Besides, you've got a very important job to do." And without

further ado, she plunged bravely into the darkness.

At first, she couldn't even see the end of her nose, and so she held out her arms to make sure she didn't bump into anything. Yet the thought of something else being in the tunnel made her even more jumpy. So to calm her nerves, Buttercup concentrated on counting each step as she went, telling herself that she'd reach the other side in no time. And sure enough, she hadn't even reached thirty when a dim glow became visible up ahead. With relief, she quickened her pace, and seconds later she emerged from the thicket to find herself standing in a clearing.

Chapter Four
A Magical Place

Buttercup gasped. For nothing could have prepared her for the magnificent sight that met her eyes.

The circular glade was bathed in shimmering light from the perfect disc of pearly moon that hung in the night sky. All around the perimeter were multicolored stalls adorned with garlands of fragrant

flowers and displaying goods of every description. Everywhere Buttercup looked there were Flower Fairies chattering happily away—some that she knew and was glad to see and others that she'd never seen before, but all of them friendly and welcoming. The most exquisite scent hung in the air—the delicate perfume of the flowers mingled with spices and herbs and things fresh from the oven. Above the hum of cheery voices came the sound of chiming bells. And there, in the very center of the glade, were Harebell and

Lily-of-the-Valley, weaving gracefully in and out of an arch made entirely of entwined clematis, shaking their bells as they danced.

Mesmerized, Buttercup slowly began to move from stall to stall. The first table she stopped at was piled high with lusciously ripe summer fruits, while the next was laden with mouthwatering cakes and seeds; a third sold intricately carved wooden instruments, and at the fourth were the prettiest shoes that Buttercup had ever seen, all lined up in neat rows. Next, she found herself drawn to a treasure chest of trinkets, baubles, and ornaments, and before she could help herself, she was

absorbed in picking out a pretty necklace
that would match her dress.

"It's Buttercup, isn't it? What are you
doing here?"

"Hmm?" replied Buttercup, still
engrossed.

"Wakey, wakey!"

With a start, Buttercup came to her senses
and looked up.

Standing in front of her was a slight fairy
dressed in a pretty white tutu skirt and a
grayish-green bodice. She looked quite wild

with her chestnut hair hanging in her eyes and her bare feet, but Buttercup knew that she lived in the Flower Fairies Garden, where her ordered flowers lived in the borders closest to the human house. It was Pink.

"Hello! Sorry—I didn't mean to ignore you. I was making an important decision." Buttercup laughed, nodding toward the collection of accessories that she had been sorting through.

"I understand," replied Pink good-naturedly. "It's wonderful here, isn't it? My brother and I always come with Tansy. We make the finishing touches to her dresses with our pinking shears." She pulled out a pair of the special scissors that cut zigzag edges into hems or cuffs and gave her flowers their unique crinkly appearance. "But I haven't seen you here before. Have you got a stall this time?"

"No, I just . . . Oh dear, I've forgotten why I'm here . . ." Buttercup had become so entranced by her new surroundings that she'd completely lost sight of her mission. "Listen, Pink—I've got to go. I'll explain later!" she called over her shoulder as she began to push her way through the throng.

There appeared to be double the amount of fairies that there had been when Buttercup arrived, and since she wasn't very tall, she couldn't see over their heads to the other side of the clearing. *What if I'm too late?* she said to herself, frantically searching for something to stand on. It would take far too long to visit each individual stall, and since everyone was moving around, she'd never be able to make sure she'd checked the whole glade for the elves.

Short of standing on a table and drawing attention to herself, Buttercup couldn't see anything immediate that would give her the height that she needed. Her heart began to race, and the palms of her hands felt clammy as she hunted for a solution. As she loosened the collar on her cloak and then lifted her arms to get some air underneath it, she realized how ridiculous she was being.

I've got wings, of course! She took a couple

of steps back to the
edge of the clearing
where the shadow of
the trees would obscure her.
Then, throwing the cloak to
the ground, she beat her wings,
and seconds later was hovering just above
the crowd.

Now although elves are similar creatures to
Flower Fairies—in that they, too, are no more
than four inches high—if you look closely,
there are some obvious differences. Their
wings and ears are extra pointy, they have
muddy bare feet and unkempt straggly hair,
and they are never without their pointed
green hats. Jack had said that the naughty
elves he'd overheard were plotting to
disguise themselves, but Buttercup felt sure
that they wouldn't be clever enough to cover

up all of their telltale features.

She'd been scanning the crowd for a good five minutes now, but to no avail. She kept spotting someone, thinking she'd found an elf, and then get a proper look and recognize them as a Flower Fairy.

"Aha! Look at *those* pointed ears—that must be one of them. Nope, patterned wings—it's Herb Robert. What about ... No, I know that face well—it's Periwinkle."

And then there was Snapdragon and Cornflower, Crocus and Honeysuckle ... It was hopeless. Buttercup felt defeated.

With a heavy heart, she admitted to herself that she'd made a mistake. "I should never have tried to sort this out on my own," she said, her eyes filling with tears. "There's nothing else for it. I shall just have to tell the others how foolish I've been."

Buttercup had just begun to look around for her friend Lily when she was distracted by a tantalizing smell drifting up from the stall below her. She glanced down. There—in an eye-catching scarlet dress—was Poppy, setting out bowls of toasted seeds coated in sticky nectar. It was her infamous popcorn that no one could resist!

And neither could this hungry, tired Flower Fairy. She landed lightly on the ground and hurried to join the line that was already forming. Her mouth watering, Buttercup waited patiently for her turn, ready to hand over the single fairy coin that she had in her skirt pocket.

Just then, her attention was caught by the two fairies who were talking loudly at the front of the line. She didn't recognize them, but their clothes seemed very familiar ... They both wore green leaf shirts with flamboyant collars and irregular hems paired with russet breeches and ... *Sycamore?* Poppy had just finished piling two bowls high with

popcorn, and one of the fairies was reaching
into a basket that hung on the far side of him.

Hang on a minute. Something about them
bothered Buttercup, and she desperately
tried to work out what it was. She didn't

know the Tree Fairy very well, but she was certain that he didn't have a brother. And—that was it—Sycamore definitely didn't wear a hat! It had to be the elves!

"Excuse me, excuse me. Sorry for pushing, but it's very important. You have to trust me—" Buttercup's heart was racing as she began nudging her way to the front as politely as she could without making a scene.

"Well," Poppy was saying, examining the pile of soft, gleaming powder that the elf held out in his cupped hands. "This is a very irregular way to be paid and it still leaves me with all the grinding to do, but it's always good to have an extra supply of fairy—"

"Wait!" shouted Buttercup. Without knowing it, Poppy was about to give away the one secret most prized by the whole of Flower Fairyland!

Chapter Five
Out of the Blue

"What on earth's the matter?" said Poppy, taken aback by the sudden disturbance.

"It's them! They're, they're..." Buttercup stammered, lost for words as it suddenly occurred to her that it would take too long to explain what was going on.

The elves seemed to have caught on to the fact that their cover was blown. The elf who'd offered Poppy the pollen was hastily brushing it off his hands into the chestnut-shell basket while the other was already backing away from the stall,

looking sheepish. It wouldn't take them a moment to slip away, and not only would it be the last that Buttercup saw of her pollen, but surely once all of the elves put their heads together they'd discover its magical properties before too long. She was going to have to do something—and fast! But what? All the fairies were talking at once now, and there was such a din that she couldn't think straight.

Just then, a long deep note resonated. It cut through the hullabaloo and stopped everyone, including the elves, in their tracks. Buttercup spun around. There, entering the glade, was a grand procession led by a fairy dressed in burgundy and

48

royal blue and blowing a horn. It was Bugle
announcing the arrival of Kingcup and
Queen of the Meadow!

As the eager Flower Fairies huddled back against the stalls to enable the regal visitors to make their way into the center of the clearing, Buttercup found herself face-to-face with the elf carrying her basket. His eyes widened as he took a good look at her and, realizing who she was, clutched the chestnut shell close to his chest so that the gold pollen reflected on his usually sallow skin. It was at that moment that Buttercup remembered something.

When it came to pollen, elves and humans had one thing in common. Of course, it would involve sacrificing every last speck of her precious harvest, but it would mean that the Flower

Fairies' secret remained safe.

It didn't take Buttercup a second to make up her mind. Taking the deepest breath she could manage, she stepped toward the elf and blew with all her might. The force of the puff lifted the pollen clean out of the basket and sent it flying straight into the elf's face. There was a moment in which he looked surprised, and then his nose began to twitch . . . and then he let out an enormous sneeze.

"*Aaa-choo!*" Followed by another even louder one. "*AAA-CHOO!*" And before he could stop himself, the elf was having a sneezing fit and everyone had turned their attention from the king and queen of

51

Flower Fairyland to the impostor in their midst. You see, some humans and *all* elves are allergic to pollen, whereas fairies don't even know *how* to sneeze!

"Elves!" Poppy exclaimed. "Oh my goodness, Buttercup—that's what you were trying to tell me. But how did you know?"

Buttercup glanced at the assembly of fairies gathered around her and blushed. It was time that she explained what a horrible mess she had got herself into. "Well, Cowslip and I got up very early this morning ..." she began.

"So, this must be the culprit," a booming voice interrupted.

And there, approaching Poppy's stall, was Kingcup, arm-in-arm with Queen of the Meadow. At this, Buttercup's knees gave way beneath her, and, bursting into tears, she sat down hard on the ground.

Chapter Six

Most Precious of All

Queen of the Meadow had the most gentle
expression that Buttercup had ever seen. She
wasn't at all as the young Flower Fairy had
expected. Her feet were bare, her gown was
a plain sleeveless smock, and on her head
she wore no crown. Her face was framed
with a cloud of blonde hair, and around
her neck was a string of simple green seeds.
But she had a natural elegance about her
and a calming presence
that made her seem
incredibly wise.

She had surprised
Buttercup by
sinking to the
ground herself

and putting a comforting arm around her. "Now, now," she said kindly. "Dry your eyes. There's nothing at all for you to be upset about. You stopped the elves from getting away with more of their usual mischief."

When Queen of the Meadow put it like that, it made things sound very straightforward, but Buttercup thought she was just being nice. She glanced up at Kingcup, too shy to meet the handsome king's gaze.

"But, Your Majesty called me a culprit—and I am." Her lip trembled, and she fought back a whole new batch of tears. "I mean," she said, lowering her voice, "I may have stopped the elves from actually getting away with my pollen, but it was my fault that they had it in the first place. My carelessness nearly caused a catastrophe for the whole of Flower Fairyland."

At that, Kingcup roared with laughter. "I wasn't calling *you* a culprit! I was talking about that roguish fellow!" he exclaimed, cocking his head in the direction of the elf, who had collapsed in a heap at the edge of the glade after his violent sneezing fit. "No, you're to be congratulated both on your quick thinking and your selflessness. You've done very well."

For the first time since that morning, Buttercup almost felt like smiling, but she hadn't told them quite everything yet.

"Yes, but it was stupid of me to try and sort it all out on my own. I was too embarrassed to ask for help, and I stopped Jack from coming to warn you." She looked

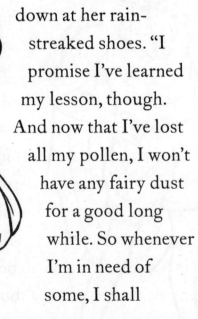

down at her rain-streaked shoes. "I promise I've learned my lesson, though. And now that I've lost all my pollen, I won't have any fairy dust for a good long while. So whenever I'm in need of some, I shall

remember that it is entirely my own fault."

There was a chuckle, and when Buttercup looked up, she saw that Queen of the Meadow had joined in with Kingcup's laughter. "Oh, my dear, you are very honest and sweet, but aren't you forgetting how generous Flower Fairies are?" she said. "You just wait and see, but I don't think it'll be long before you're busy making your own fairy dust again!"

Poppy had retrieved Buttercup's cloak and given her a bowl of her delectable popcorn and a cup of chamomile tea. She sat and chatted to her whenever there was a lull at

her stall and, despite not knowing exactly what the queen meant, Buttercup began to feel quite cheerful.

The elves had been sent home after a

stern telling-off, but Kingcup and Queen of the Meadow—who came from the marshes, too—were used to their antics and assured everyone that really they meant no harm. Besides, after all that terrible sneezing, it seemed unlikely that they'd go near any pollen for a long time! Then, as Bugle started up a tune on his horn, the king took the queen

by the hand and led her to the center of the
clearing, and soon the glade was filled with
whirling, twirling Flower Fairies.

Buttercup was too exhausted by the
day's events to join in the festivities, but she
happily watched. She was determined not to
miss any aspect of the magical fair but, as the
dancing gave way to tranquil singing, she felt
her eyelids becoming heavier and heavier,
and soon she was struggling to stop them
from closing.

"Buttercup."

A soft voice broke into the Flower Fairy's dream, and when she opened her eyes it took her a moment to get her bearings. Lily-of-the-Valley was standing in front of her. *Where was she?*

Then she noticed the hive of activity behind her friend and realized that she was still in the glade and must have drifted off to sleep. Fingers of gray were creeping into the dark sky as dawn approached and everyone was busily packing up the fair.

Lily smiled. "I've got something to show you—come on." And, beckoning for Buttercup to follow, she darted ahead and

disappeared into a nearby copse.

The sky was rapidly changing now, moving through a kaleidoscope of pink and orange hues, until eventually it settled on the clean blue of a new day.

"Look—over there," Lily said, pointing toward a pine tree that had just emerged from the gloom. "Go on," she added reassuringly.

Buttercup followed her gaze—and there, at the base of the tree, was a patch of bright yellow flowers. Buttercups! She couldn't believe her eyes! And wait ... there also appeared to be what looked like a scroll of parchment.

"It's for you," Lily

said, smiling broadly. "Now, I've got to go and help the others, but come and find me when you're ready to go back to your meadow." And without giving Buttercup a chance to ask what was going on, the light-footed fairy opened her wings and fluttered

off toward the clearing.

Not knowing what to expect, the young Flower Fairy hesitated for a few seconds. Then, with trembling hands, she picked up the parchment, unrolled it, and began to read:

Dear Buttercup

We, the undersigned, promise that all of us will search our own corner of Flower Fairyland until we find some more buttercups. When we do, each one of us will bring you a parcel of pollen to help you make your own special fairy dust.

Your friends forever,

Lily, Poppy, Crocus, Honeysuckle, Harebell, Tansy, Pink, Snapdragon

(and so the list went on)

"This is what Queen of the Meadow
meant!" Buttercup gasped.

Completely overwhelmed, she sat down
on the woodland floor and reflected for a
moment on all that had happened to her

since Cowslip had woken her the previous
morning.

As she watched the first rays of sunshine
light up the clump of golden buttercups,
she felt glad that she would have some of

her beloved pollen after all. Yet, glancing down at the parchment that was still in her hands, Buttercup realized that she had just learned the real meaning of fairy gold. The most precious thing a Flower Fairy could ever have was friends—and no matter how hard they tried, that was something the elves would never be able to steal!